PUFFIN BOOKS

SAUSAGE MOLE AND LI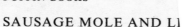

Lucas the horse shares his field and his stable with a mole – a sausage mole! Lucas lives above the ground and Mole lives underneath. Mole digs lots of tunnels that sometimes come up in the most surprising places, much to Lucas's annoyance. But despite everything the two are very good friends until they fall out over food – or to be more precise Mole's favourite food – sausage rolls!

In the second story Mole and Lucas have a new friend. A little foal comes to join them and both Mole and Lucas help Little Foal get over his fear of dark and stormy nights.

Diane Redmond has written several books, but this is her first Young Puffin. She also writes children's plays and television scripts. She lives in Cambridge with her husband, three children and a horse called Lucas!

Diane Redmond

Sausage Mole
and Little Foal

Illustrated by John Eastwood

PUFFIN BOOKS

For Tamsin, my Big Girl, and Lucas himself

PUFFIN BOOKS

Published by the Penguin Group
Penguin Books Ltd, 27 Wrights Lane, London W8 5TZ, England
Penguin Books USA Inc., 375 Hudson Street, New York, New York 10014, USA
Penguin Books Australia Ltd, Ringwood, Victoria, Australia
Penguin Books Canada Ltd, 10 Alcorn Avenue, Toronto, Ontario, Canada M4V 3B2
Penguin Books (NZ) Ltd, 182–190 Wairau Road, Auckland 10, New Zealand

Penguin Books Ltd, Registered Offices: Harmondsworth, Middlesex, England

First published by Viking 1991
Published in Puffin Books 1993
10 9 8 7 6 5 4 3 2

Text copyright © Diane Redmond, 1991
Illustrations copyright © John Eastwood, 1991
All rights reserved

The moral right of the author has been asserted

Printed in England by Clays Ltd, St Ives plc
Filmset in Times (Linotron 202)

Contents

1. Sausage Mole

Lucas and Mole live in a big field on the edge of a busy town. They're friends now, but when they first met they didn't like each other at all.

It all started one afternoon when Lucas was eating the grass under the horse-chestnut tree.

Mole suddenly popped up

and yelled: "Hey, you. Clear off!"

Lucas snorted and stamped his hoof. "Dung Heaps!" he neighed. "I live here."

"You may live on top," said Mole, "but I live underneath and I'm sick of you flattening my tunnels with your great, clod-hopping feet!"

Lucas couldn't believe his ears.

"What do you want me to do?" he asked. "Move out?"

"No, you can stay," bossed Mole. "As long as you stop bothering me!"

And without another word, he shot back down his hole.

"Cheeky little squirt!" said Lucas.

But the very next night, Mole turned up in Lucas's

stable. Lucas was fast asleep
when something furry tickled
his ear.

"HAH! What's that?" he
cried and scrambled to his feet.

SCRATCH! SCRATCH!
SCRATCH!

Somebody was digging a
hole in his stable floor.

"Come out, or I'll jump on
you," said Lucas.

"OOOOH! Don't do that,"
squeaked Mole and crept out,
covered in straw.

"I'm sorry," he said. "I've
been burrowing a new hole all
day and I couldn't find my way
out."

Mole yawned and rubbed his little brown whiskers. "Dear me, I'm so tired," he sighed.

"You'd better stay, now that you're here," said Lucas.

"Thanks," said Mole, snuggling up close and cosy. "Night, night, sleep tight. Don't let the bedbugs bite!" he giggled.

"Night, Mole," said Lucas, and that's how they became best friends.

The trouble with Mole is that he never stops eating. He eats everything. Weeds, worms, beetles, pony nuts and sausage rolls.

"SAUSAGE ROLLS!" laughed Lucas. "Moles don't eat sausage rolls."

"I do," said Mole.

Mole loves sausage rolls, but in the week they are very hard to find.

Weekends are better, when the Big Girl comes.

Big and noisy, loud and bossy, she drives Mole mad.

Mucking out, tacking up, grooming down, she's a pain in the neck.

But she brings the sausage rolls.

She always leaves them in the tack-box with a flask of tea and a packet of mints, and for months Mole has feasted on them.

Crisp and buttery, light and airy, with a salty, pink sausage filling.

"Mmmmmmmm!"

He just can't get enough of them.

"You'll cop it," said Lucas.
"No I won't," said Mole.
"She'll think you eat them."
"HUMPH!" snorted Lucas.
"As if a horse would eat
sausage rolls!"

15

But as the weeks went by, the Big Girl did think that Lucas was eating her sausage rolls.

"I don't know where they go," she grumbled. "Is it you?" she asked him.

Lucas shook his head and flicked his tail crossly.

"Dung Heaps! I'm a vegetarian!" he snorted and buried his head in a bucket of oats.

When the sausage rolls disappeared for the *seventeenth* time, the Big Girl decided it was time to take action.

"It takes a spy to catch a spy," she said and hid behind the stable wall, waiting for the thief!

Mole was half-way up his hole, heading straight for the sausage rolls, when he heard Lucas neighing very loudly.

"Oh-oh! Trouble!" he squeaked and immediately about-turned and scampered back down the tunnel.

He popped up just in front of the stable and saw the Big Girl

sitting on a bucket, with her face pressed up against the stable wall.

"Hah!" thought Mole. "Two can play at that game!"

He sat behind her, watching and waiting, and smiled.

"I bet she gets fed up before I do!" he thought, and she did.

After half an hour she kicked the bucket clear across the field.

"I'm going to get to the bottom of this!" she cried.

She stormed back into the stable and turned it upside down.

"Just wait till I get my hands

on that thief!" she muttered.
But she didn't find anything.
Not a rat, a dog or a cat. It

wasn't an owl or a stoat or a
weasel, and she never saw the
mole-hole because Lucas
stamped his hoof right on top
of it.

She got hot and cross and
then she gave up.

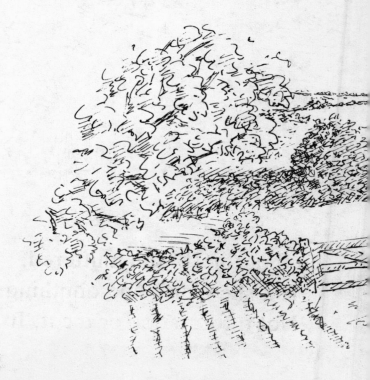

"Come on, boy," she said to Lucas. "Let's go out for a ride."

She saddled him up and galloped off up the lane.

Clip-clop, clip-clop, clip-clop, clip.

"Yippee!" cried Mole. "Now for lunch!"

He dived back down his tunnel and thundered along the winding passageways, his tummy rumbling for sausage rolls.

"Let me at 'em!" he drooled.

Seconds later he came up in Lucas's stable. There they were – three of them this week.

"Mmmmmm-muph!" slurped Mole as he sunk his teeth into the light, crisp, buttery pastry.

"Aahhh!" he sighed as he bit into the salty sausage filling. "This beats worms any day!"

Mole walloped back the

three sausage rolls then lay
down, stuffed to the ears.

"Now for a little snooze," he
yawned. "Z-Z-Z-Z-Z-Z!"

Lucas came trotting back
and woke him up. "You'll cop
it!" he grumbled.

Mole licked his whiskers and
burped. "No I won't," he said.

"I bet you a bag of pony nuts you'll cop it before the week's out," said Lucas.

"And I bet you a sausage roll I won't!" said Mole and swaggered off, too full to argue.

But Lucas was right.

Mole *did* cop it the next weekend.

After he'd swiped the sausage rolls for the *eighteenth* time, the Big Girl went mad.

"OK, that's *it*!" she fumed. "I'm going to block up all the holes in the stable."

"She can't do that," hissed Mole. "I live here!"

"She can do what she wants," said Lucas. "She pays the rent."

The Big Girl stuffed rubbish down every hole and jumped on it.

BONG! BONG! BONG!

"There, that'll teach *you* a lesson, you little rat!" she bellowed.

Mole was furious.

"Doesn't she know the difference between a mole and a rat?" he grumbled.

"She soon will!" laughed Lucas.

"Well, I'm not going to be bunged up!" said Mole, and he started to dig more tunnels. He made a spaghetti junction of loops and tracks and freeways that came up in the most unexpected places.

"Mole! I'm sick to the back teeth of you!" fumed Lucas. "I

can't budge an inch without falling down one of your blinkin' holes. Pack it in!"

"Pack it in?" gasped Mole. "You can't be serious! I *have* to have more routes to get to my sausage rolls!"

"Huh! I like that," scoffed Lucas. "Your sausage rolls – they're *hers*. You steal them, Mole, you're a thief!"

Mole stamped his foot. "How dare you call *me* a thief!"

"You are – and you're ruining my stable. Just look at the mess you've made!"

Mole was furious.

"What about me?" he raged.
"Every time I turn around I've
got one of your great,
clod-hopping hoofs poking
through my ceiling. Honestly,

you're ruining my brilliant tunnel system."

"Let's get one thing straight," snapped Lucas. "I *live* here, you're just a lodger!"

"W-H-A-T! Me, a lodger?" exploded Mole. "I've never been so insulted in my life!"

The two friends glared at each other.

"Well, that's it," said Mole. "I know when I'm not wanted."

"You're definitely *not* wanted," said Lucas and stamped his foot on the ground.

"YIKES!" he whinnied and
for the third time that day he
slipped down a mole-hole.
"Get out!" he roared.

"I will," said Mole, walking
off with his nose in the air.
"And I'm not coming back!"

"Good riddance to bad
rubbish," neighed Lucas.

"And the same to you, with
knobs on!" yelled Mole.

But after two days, Lucas
missed Mole and Mole missed
Lucas.

Mole also missed the sausage
rolls!

After five days of sulking
they both wanted to be friends,
but neither of them would
make the first move. Then they

bumped into each other by the water-trough.

"How's life?" asked Lucas.

"Can't grumble," answered Mole. "Anything been going on up here?"

"Lots," said Lucas, and before they knew it they were off, chatting to each other about the weather, the worms, the weeds and the world in general.

"I might pop in tomorrow," said Mole.

Lucas smiled. "I thought you might," he said. "Tomorrow's Saturday, sausage day, right?"

"Maybe," answered Mole

and looked uncomfortable.

"Well, you won't find any," said Lucas.

"Go on," said Mole, "you're pulling my leg."

"I'm not," said Lucas. "The Big Girl's gone vegetarian."

"I don't believe you!" laughed Mole.

"It's the truth," said Lucas. "She eats spring rolls and vegetable samosas these days."

"No!" gasped Mole.

"Come and see for yourself!" laughed Lucas.

"I will!" said Mole.

The next day when the Big Girl came, Mole hid under the

hay and watched her put her
lunch in the tack-box, just as
usual. But something was
wrong.

"It smells funny," thought
Mole.

39

He waited for her to leave.
As soon as he heard the
clip-clop of Lucas's hoofs in the
lane, he belted across the
stable and wriggled into the
tack-box.

"Sausage rolls, whoopee!"
he cried.

But Lucas was right, the Big
Girl had gone vegetarian. All
that Mole could find was a
spring roll and two vegetable
samosas.

"POOOH! What a pong!"
he cried. "Maybe they taste
better than they smell!"

He tried a samosa first and
his mouth nearly lit up.

"AGHH!" he yelled and dived head-first into Lucas's water-bucket.

"Great balls of fire!" he gasped. "That's H-O-T! Maybe the spring roll will be better."

It was all wet and slimy.

"YUK! Just like grass," spluttered Mole and spat it out.

He threw the food back into the tack-box and stomped off.

"Give me worms any day!" sniffed Mole.

When Lucas came back, Mole was finishing off a long, cool, slippery worm.

"What do you think of the new stuff?" asked Lucas.

"R-E-V-O-L-T-I-N-G!" cried Mole.

"That's a relief," sighed Lucas. "Maybe we'll have a bit of peace round here now."

The Big Girl ate her

vegetarian lunch, then went off to meet her noisy friend in the village.

Mole and Lucas settled down by the water-trough and watched the world go by.

"Nice to be back to normal again," said Mole.

"Very nice," agreed Lucas. "But I'll tell you something," sighed Mole. "I'll never, *ever* forget those wonderful sausage rolls!"

2. Little Foal

When the Big Girl took her
horse-box across the field,
Mole went mad.

"She'll flatten all my holes,"
he squeaked.

"Don't worry, you can build
some more," said Lucas.
"Come on, let's go and see
who the visitor is."

"Visitors!" sniffed Mole. "I
hate visitors."

A pretty little foal popped
her head out of the horse-box
and whinnied nervously.

"She's frightened," said Lucas.

"Who-aah!" said the Big Girl. "Whoa-ah there."

The little foal wouldn't come out of the box. She kept rearing up and hitting herself on the railing.

"Lucas, come and help me," called the Big Girl.

Lucas walked calmly up the ramp and sniffed the little foal.

"Hello, there," he said. "What's your name?"

The little foal stared at him with big brown eyes. "I don't have a name," she said. "My mum just called me Baby."

"Well, you're a big girl
now," said Lucas. "Come out
and I'll show you around."

"I'm scared," whispered the
little foal.

"Don't worry," said Lucas.
"There's nothing to be
frightened of."

He walked down the ramp
and the little foal quickly
skipped after him.

"Well done!" cried the Big Girl. "Lucas will look after you."

The little foal frisked about in the sunshine.

"Will you really look after me?" she asked.

"Of course I will," said Lucas. "We're all friends here."

"HUMPH!" said Mole, digging his hole. "Some of us are!"

Lucas showed the little foal the stable, the water-trough, the jumps and the paddock. Then he took her all around the edges of the field so that she could see the park and the river on the other side of the fences.

"This is where Mole lives," said Lucas as they passed his hole.

Mole popped out and looked at the little foal.

"Pleased to meet you, Mr Mole," she said politely and Mole suddenly smiled.

"At least you've not got clod-hopping feet like some horses I could mention," he said.

Lucas winked at the little foal. He knew they were all going to get along just fine.

The little foal was small and white with a silver mane and tail. She followed Lucas around like a shadow.

"I'll call you Silver Shadow," said the Big Girl.

"That's a fancy name for a little thing like you," said Mole.

"We'll call you Little Foal," said Lucas.

"Good, I like that best," said Little Foal, and that's how she got her name.

Little Foal did everything with Lucas.

They ate their breakfast and supper together, they grazed in

the paddock together, they
even slept in the same stable
every night.

Lucas taught her everything
he knew. How to walk and
trot, jump and canter. He even

washed her ears when they
were dirty and dried her face
when she got wet in the rain.

"You'll spoil her," said
Mole, but he was just as bad.

He showed her where to find
the sweetest grass and the
coolest water.

He licked her legs when
she'd been stung by nettles,
and when it was very hot he
put elderflower leaves around
her eyes, to keep the flies
away.

They both loved Little Foal
and she loved them.

Then one day the thunder came.

B-O-O-O-M!

It rattled across the sky all afternoon and Little Foal was terrified.

"AH! OOH! What's that?"
she whinnied.

"Thunder," explained Lucas.
"It's up there, in the sky. It'll
pass over soon, you'll see."

But it didn't pass over. It got worse and worse.

C-R-A-C-K! B-O-O-M! B-O-O-M!

Little Foal reared up and hit herself against the stable wall.

"AH!" she cried and buried her head against Lucas's shoulder.

"Dear, dear, what are we going to do with her?" worried Mole.

"I don't know," said Lucas, eyeing the dark storm clouds. "It looks like it's set in for the night."

When the Big Girl heard the

thunder, she rushed to the
stable to see if Little Foal and
Lucas were all right.

The rain was lashing down,
lightning was zigzagging across
the sky and Little Foal was
crashing all over the stable,
neighing at the top of her
voice.

"Goodness, she's in an awful state," said the Big Girl.

She took hold of the pony and tried to stroke her, but Little Foal bucked and started kicking the stable door.

"I'd better move her before she hurts herself," said the Big Girl.

"*No!* Leave her here, she'll be frightened on her own," neighed Lucas.

"Now don't you start making a fuss," said the Big Girl. "I've enough on my hands with Silver Shadow."

Lucas watched her lead Little Foal into the empty

stable at the bottom of the
field.

"Follow them!" he cried,
stamping his hoof on Mole's
hole.

"I'll do my best," promised
Mole and scampered off as fast
as his little legs would carry
him.

The Big Girl put a blanket
on Little Foal and made her a
warm bran-mash.

"Good night," she said.
"Sleep well."

As soon as the Big Girl had
gone, Little Foal went wild.

"I WANT LUCAS!" she
neighed.

"STOP IT!" yelled Mole as
Little Foal ran around the
stable, rolling her eyes.

B-O-O-M! roared the
thunder.

Z-I-P! went the lightning.

"AHH!" squealed Little
Foal and jumped right over the
stable door.

"COME BACK!" yelled
Mole. "C-O-M-E
B-A-C-K!"

But Little Foal was off,
galloping across the field with
her silver mane flying out
behind her.

"STOP!" neighed Lucas as
she flashed by, but she headed

for the fence and jumped right
over it.

"Lucas, help!" shouted
Mole. "HELP!"

Lucas was stuck in his stable, with the door bolted.

"Dung Heaps!" he cried and kicked at the door until it fell off its hinges.

"She went that way!" cried Mole, pointing towards the busy High Street.

"Grab my tail and hold on tight," said Lucas and galloped down the High Street after her.

Lightning flashed and thunder rolled as they pounded through the night.

Cars screeched to a halt and honked their horns when they saw the runaway horses.

Suddenly blue lights flashed

and sirens sounded.

DEE-DAW. DEE-DAW. DEE-DAW!

Lucas stopped and hid behind a tree on the village green.

"Oh, my goodness, I hope she's not been run over," he said.

Mole crept close to get a better view.

"Can you see her?" whispered Lucas.

"Yes," said Mole, sneaking around a woman's foot. "She looks very frightened."

"Is she hurt?" asked Lucas.

"No, but the police are taking her away," said Mole.

The police put Little Foal in a field at the back of the police station.

"Boo-hoo-hoo!" she cried when they left her on her own.

"Shshsh!" said Lucas. "We'll look after you."

"N-E-I-G-H!" squealed Little Foal when she saw her friends. "Please stay with me, don't go away."

"We'll stay till morning, then we'll have to go home to fetch the Big Girl," said Lucas.

As soon as it was light,

Lucas galloped back to the field with Mole clinging to his tail.

"Shadow's gone!" cried the Big Girl, when she looked into the empty stable. "Come on, Lucas," she said. "We've got to find her right away."

She quickly tacked Lucas up and trotted him out into the High Street, but instead of turning left she turned right.

"Oh, no!" thought Lucas and tried to turn around the other way.

"Stop it!" shouted the Big Girl, tugging the bit and digging her heels into his side.

"Walk on, walk on."

Lucas had no intention of walking on.

Even if it meant getting into trouble, he was determined to go to the police station.

He spun round on his back legs and trotted back the way they'd come.

"LUCAS! What is the matter with you?" yelled the Big Girl.

"You'll soon find out," thought Lucas, and breaking into a canter he headed straight for the police station.

"WHEEE-EEEE!" called Little Foal when she saw Lucas and the Big Girl.

"SHADOW!" cried the Big Girl. "What are *you* doing here?"

"She nearly got run over last night," said the policeman. "We had to put her somewhere safe, so we locked her in our field."

"Thank you," said the Big Girl, shaking the policeman's hand. "You probably saved her life."

When they were out in the lane, the Big Girl hugged Lucas.

"Thank you too, you clever boy," she said. "You knew where she was, didn't you?"

Lucas lifted his head and neighed loudly. "Of course I did," he said.

"Well done," said the Big Girl and at last they all set off for home.

That night Mole, Lucas and Little Foal lay down in the

stable together and listened to
the sound of the wind sighing
in the tree-tops.

"I won't ever run away
again," said Little Foal,

snuggling up close to her
friends.

"Good!" said Lucas.

"Night," yawned Mole.

But Little Foal was fast
asleep. "Z-Z-Z-Z-Z-Z-Z!"
she snored.

She'd had enough excitement
for one day!